W9-BRD-161

09/04/07 Childs World

Seasons and Weather
Las Estaciones y El Tiempo

by Mary Berendes • illustrated by Kathleen Petelinsek

Published in the United States of America by The Child's World®
1980 Lookout Drive • Mankato, MN 56003-1705
800-599-READ • www.childsworld.com

Acknowledgments
The Child's World®: Mary Berendes, Publishing Director
The Design Lab: Kathleen Petelinsek, Design and Page Production

Language Adviser: Ariel Strichartz

Library of Congress Cataloging-in-Publication Data
Berendes, Mary.
  Seasons and weather = Las estaciones y el tiempo / by Mary Berendes;
illustrated by Kathleen Petelinsek.
      p. cm. — (Wordbooks = Libros de palabras)
  ISBN-13: 978-1-59296-801-5 (library bound: alk. paper)
  ISBN-10: 1-59296-801-5 (alk. paper)
  1. Seasons—Juvenile literature. 2. Weather—Juvenile literature.
I. Petelinsek, Kathleen, ill. II. Title. III. Title: Las Estaciones y El tiempo.
  QB637.4.B47 2007
  508.2—dc22   2006103384

spring
la primavera

bee
la abeja

tulip
el tulipán

dirt
la tierra

rabbit
el conejo

3

rainbow
el arco iris

birds
los pájaros

rain
la lluvia

4

cloud
la nube

umbrella
el paraguas

duck
el pato

pocket
el bolsillo

frog
la rana

boots
las galochas

6

splash
salpicar

showers
los chubascos

raindrop
la gota de
lluvia

raincoat
el impermeable

boat
el barco

puddle
el charco

7

sun
el sol

beach ball
la pelota de playa

towel
la toalla

swimsuit
el traje de baño

water toy
el juguete acuático

8

summer
el verano

jump
saltar

diving board
el trampolín

pool
la piscina

swim
nadar

9

shore
la orilla

lake
el lago

ducks
los patos

bobber
el flotador

oranges
las naranjas

tree
el árbol

trunk
el tronco

fishing pole
la caña
de pescar

oar
el remo

boat
el barco

worms
los gusanos

11

lightning
el relámpago

tornado
el tornado

storm
la tormenta

house
la casa

city
la ciudad

13

wind
el viento

leaves
las hojas

14

autumn
el otoño

sweater
el suéter

rake
el rastrillo

15

palm trees
las palmeras

hurricane
el huracán

island
la isla

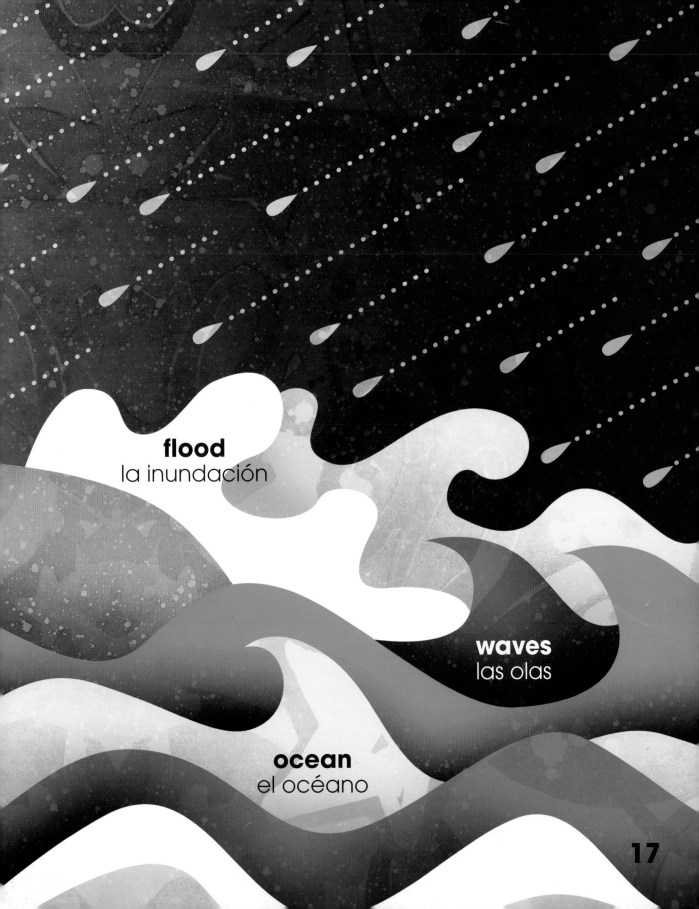

flood
la inundación

waves
las olas

ocean
el océano

17

branches
las ramas

snow
la nieve

winter
el invierno

hat
el sombrero

carrot
la zanahoria

mittens
los mitones

scarf
la bufanda

snowman
el muñeco
de nieve

19

icicles
las carámbanos

frost
la escarcha

snowflakes
los copos
de nieve

drift
el ventisquero

blizzard
la ventisca

21

pine trees
los pinos

ice
el hielo

22

snowbank
el montículo
de nieve

ice-skate
patinar
sobre hielo

23

word list
lista de palabras

English	Spanish	English	Spanish
autumn	el otoño	**pool**	la piscina
beach ball	la pelota de playa	**puddle**	el charco
bee	la abeja	**rabbit**	el conejo
birds	los pájaros	**rain**	la lluvia
blizzard	la ventisca	**rainbow**	el arco iris
boat	el barco	**raincoat**	el impermeable
bobber	el flotador	**raindrop**	la gota de lluvia
boots	las galochas	**rake**	el rastrillo
branches	las ramas	**scarf**	la bufanda
carrot	la zanahoria	**seasons**	las estaciones
city	la ciudad	**shore**	la orilla
cloud	la nube	**showers**	los chubascos
dirt	la tierra	**snow**	la nieve
diving board	el trampolín	**snowbank**	el montículo de nieve
duck	el pato	**snowdrift**	el ventisquero
fishing pole	la caña de pescar	**snowflakes**	los copos de nieve
flood	la inundación	**snowman**	el muñeco de nieve
frog	la rana	**(to) splash**	salpicar
frost	la escarcha	**spring**	la primavera
hat	el sombrero	**storm**	la tormenta
house	la casa	**summer**	el verano
hurricane	el huracán	**sun**	el sol
ice	el hielo	**sweater**	el suéter
(to) ice-skate	patinar sobre hielo	**swim**	nadar
icicles	las carámbanos	**swimsuit**	el traje de baño
island	la isla	**tornado**	el tornado
jump	saltar	**towel**	la toalla
lake	el lago	**tree**	el árbol
leaves	las hojas	**trunk**	el tronco
lightning	el relámpago	**tulip**	el tulipán
mittens	los mitones	**umbrella**	el paraguas
oar	el remo	**water toy**	el juguete acuático
ocean	el océano	**waves**	las olas
oranges	las naranjas	**weather**	el tiempo
palm trees	las palmeras	**wind**	el viento
pine trees	los pinos	**winter**	el invierno
pocket	el bolsillo	**worms**	los gusanos